The death of D
By K.N. Par

1
An Unexpected Visitor

One dreary night, a small, slim figure draped all in black arrived in a room rather inconspicuously in a cloud of dark smoke and what can only be described as dozens of little sparks, quite like the sparks you see when you touch someone or something after rubbing your sock covered feet on a shaggy rug. The room the figure had just appeared in was rather dark, save for an eerie glow from a large square shaped hole, no doubt a window, in front of which sat a similar small and bald silhouette looking up into the cloudy night sky.

The figure cleared her throat before quietly calling out, "Miss Wilkinson?"

The small silhouette did not move. The figure in black tried once more.

"Tabitha? Miss Tabitha Wilkinson?"

This time the silhouette moved its head in the direction of the voice. Clearly startled, Tabitha asked, "Who's there? Is someone there?"

"Yes," a soft, ghostly voice answered back. "Someone is most definitely here. Well, I was once considered a someone at one time but I'm not quite sure I can be classified as such anymore."

The tiny silhouette stepped slowly down from the windowsill and apprehensively inched toward the direction of the voice.

"Whatever you are, you sound female. Do you know if you were female?"

"Perhaps I was," the figure in black answered rather unsurely.

"May I ask what you are doing here?"

"Certainly. But first, a little light may help our situation,"

"Oh, quite right. Let me… "

Tabitha started toward the light switch on her wall but before she was able to take a single step, a dim white glow sprang forth from two small circles and a slim slit below them. The barely bright enough light moved closer and closer toward the silhouette until it finally revealed—but only just—a young girl in sleep wear decorated in pink kitty cats and yellow stars with frilly trim, the conventional sleep wear of many a young girl her age. She had no eyebrows and no hair except for a little fuzz on the sides and a few scraggly strands on top. Her face was at that moment pale and sickly, yet sweet and pretty; the expression on it was all at once one of inquisition, fascination and terror.

The face that stared back at Tabitha's was a strange one at that. In fact, it was hardly a face at all; it strongly resembled a mask, complete with red string tied around the back. It was chalk white with no usual facial features that could be spoken of, with two small circular—and rather empty—eye sockets and a very small mouth that were now, as mentioned before, glowing with a dull white light. There was, however, one unusual feature: a crack that started from top left of her head that ended in a spider web-like pattern just above her left eye with a faint red stain in the middle. The rest of the body was as black as a shadow: a living, breathing shadow. The two were nearly identical as far as their body shapes and heights were concerned.

As the two beings finished sizing each other up, the figure in black finally spoke.

"You are a Miss Tabitha Wilkinson, are you not?"

"Yes… yes I am, but why are you…?"

"…I am here to inform you, Miss Wilkinson, of your impending death," the figure in black said, cutting Tabitha off.

"My impending what?"

"Death."

"Death? So that means… are you *the* Death?" Tabitha curiously asked, rather unshaken by the news.

"Some incorrectly refer to us as such. But that is not our official name. We are your caretakers in death. Your death guides if you will," the small figure in black answered back.

"We? Are there more of you then?" Tabitha asked, startled more by this revelation than she was of her own mortal end.

"Yes, quite a bit more of us actually."

"Death guides," Tabitha murmured to herself as she slowly and absentmindedly wandered back toward the moonlit windowsill.

A tuft of smoke that resembled a pad of paper suddenly appeared before the figure in black. Its appearance was accompanied by a sound, the kind you hear when you lay your head down quickly onto a large and especially fluffy pillow. The sound caught Tabitha's attention.

"What is that you're doing?" she asked.

"Excuse me?"

"That thing in your hands you keep looking at. That rather smoky thing,"

The figure in black slowly looked up at the girl.

"Notes," the figure answered, simply.

"Notes on what exactly?"

"I must say, Miss Wilkinson, you are taking this much better than the other clients I've had so far. The others were terrified at the mere sight of me. And they were even more upset when they learned they were going to die. But you seem to be keeping your bearings," said the figure in black, completely ignoring Tabitha's question.

Tabitha climbed onto her squeaky bed, brought her knees to her chest and wrapped them in her arms.

"Oh, I've been fairly calm all my life. Besides, you're not all that scary. And why worry about something you cannot change?"

"Exactly," the figure in black agreed.

Tabitha scooted a little closer toward the figure in black and stared at her intently as the figure looked over the pad seemingly made of smoke.

"You look kind of familiar. Where have I seen you before?"

"I haven't the faintest idea," said the guide as she continued looking over her notes. Tabitha's curiosity about something finally got the best of her.

"When shall we be going then, guide? When is my time?" asked Tabitha, with slight nervousness in her voice.

"How old are you Miss Wilkinson?" asked the figure in black.

"I will be twelve and a half by next…"

"…You will not be making it to thirteen," said the figure in black rather dryly, and interrupting once again. Tabitha gave out a slight whimper and clasped her hand to her mouth.

"Was that your attempt at comforting humor? Because if it was, you have sorely missed the mark," she said, fighting back tears.

"My apologies Miss Wilkinson. I can assure you it was not."

The figure in black, looking down at the tuft of smoke, cleared her throat once more before speaking again.

"If you will allow me to formally inform you that you, Miss Tabitha Wilkinson, are due to perish from this realm and enter the next at approximately two days from our current date, at which point I will return to collect you."

"Enter the next? The next what?" asked Tabitha, frustrated.

"Realm of course," answered the figure in black.

"What realm? How extremely vague."

"We feel that since you will experience it for yourself very soon, there is no need to go into arbitrary details at this time."

"Can I at least know your name?" asked Tabitha.

The figure in black answered back, "My name is not important,"

"Are the rest of the guides as cold as you are?" asked Tabitha. The figure in black did not have an answer for this.

"I'm going to die in two days. You could stand to be a little warmer. You are my caretaker after all," said Tabitha.

"I do not have a name as of yet," the figure in black answered, ignoring the latter question and addressing the former. "I have just begun this occupation. I am at the moment, nameless."

"Nameless," said Tabitha. The figure silently nodded her head before she started again with the rest of her prepared speech.

"We, your humble guides, advise you to use this precious time to express your final farewells to any loved ones you are able to. This includes personal possessions and pets of any kind."

As she finished, the pad of smoke vanished back into the thin air it appeared from.

"Oh, and we also advise you not to divulge this information to anyone, least of all, because they will plainly not believe you, thus avoiding any unnecessary embarrassment. You may also run the risk of causing them unneeded distress,"

"Cause them distress? I'm the one who's perishing," said Tabitha.

"What about not worrying about those things which you cannot change?"

"I am calm about it. That does mean that I do not care about it. There is a difference. Who's going to comfort me?" asked Tabitha with genuine concern.

"Loved ones of course. A dog or a fish perhaps,"

"I don't own either of those,"

"A bird then?"

Tabitha shook her head.

"How about siblings? Do you have any of those?"

Tabitha looked visibly shaken by this question. Her eyes grew very sad on her face. She slowly lowered her head and hesitated a moment before shaking it once more.

"Well, I'm sure you'll figure something…"

"I have a father and a mother. Will those do?" Tabitha spoke up.

"I do not see why they wouldn't. Now if you will excuse me," said the figure in black as she turned to leave.

"Wait!" pleaded Tabitha. "I have many more questions for you, guide,"

The figure paused for a moment before turning back around toward her.

"Yes?"

"Does everyone who dies receive a guide such as yourself?" Tabitha asked with sincerity.

"No," she said.

"Well, who then? Who is deserving of a guide?"

The figure in black took a moment before answering. She spotted a pillow on the girl's bed and briefly considered picking it up and throwing it at her if it would stop her asking questions. She did not do this. Instead, she answered her.

"Those with a similar condition such as yours mostly: Those with time. Most elderly. Those whom, with reasonable certainty, can sense their oncoming demise before anyone else around them can,"

There was pause before she spoke again.

"And those who do not receive a guide…" she started, anticipating Tabitha's next question "…are those with no time. Those who perish in freak accidents, those who perish in their sleep without warning, and those who perish due to heart attacks and strokes and other similar unavoidable medical conditions. And infants."

"Why don't infants deserve a guide?"

"Why, the inability to comprehend of course."

"Oh, of course. Are there anymore?" continued Tabitha.

"Yes, there are more but these are the primary candidates. Now, I really must be…"

"Wait, please guide. A few more questions."

The figure in black nodded, trying her hardest not to sigh audibly.

"How does one get to be in a situation such as yours? You make it sound like work. How do you get this job?" Tabitha asked innocently.

The figure in black hesitated to answer. None of her previous clients, though small in number, have ever been this inquisitive before so she never had to question herself or her own situation. She thought to herself long and hard but no simple answer to the question had entered her mind. The oldest memory she could conjure was one of approximately a month old, or, at least what seemed like a month—it may very well could have been a week, a day or simply an hour—and she remembered opening her eyes and being in a rather drab, medium-size room lacking in detail that seemed to be painted with cigarette-ash, standing in line with many similarly dressed death guides; all dressed in black from head to toe, but of varying heights and varying different faces: some rather odd and disfigured, and some with only slight blemishes, but all peculiarly familiar. She remembered standing with the rest of the guides, all of them very compliant, including herself, and all facing a figure in black, much taller and much older in appearance than any of the guides themselves, standing at the front of the room. He was giving a rather generic and, as she could judge, a much-prepared speech that included the rules and regulations of the task that they were to perform. She could not pull a memory from her mind that was older than this.

As her senses returned to the present, she looked at Tabitha and answered, "One does not apply for this position. One does not ask to be put in this situation. One just is and one just does."

"I see." Tabitha nodded in comprehension. She asked one more question before the figure had a chance to turn and leave again. "And how did you die?"

The figure stared, with what was considered to be her eyes, into Tabitha's own. "Excuse me?" she asked Tabitha.

"You said that you used to be considered someone. That implies that you were once alive. How did you die? What is your story?" Tabitha asked once again.

"I… I…" This seemed to cause the figure some distress of her own. She thought and thought but could not for the life of her, or death of her rather, conjure an answer.

"I do not have a story. I cannot remember," she finally said, and Tabitha grew sad once more.

"I really must be going, Miss Wilkinson."

"Before your next visit, guide…" Tabitha started before the figure had a chance to move "…I want you to do something for me. I want to hear your story. I want you to find out how you died and how you came to be in this position, and I also want you to find out your real name. And then I want you to tell me your findings when you return. Can you do that for me, guide?"

The guide thought to decline, she really wanted to, as this was no business of this bald and sickly little girl's. But instead, for reasons only known to her, gave a sharp and hurried nod. It was unclear whether she did so in compliance or because she was in hurry to leave, but Tabitha seemed satisfied with the response.

"So, I'll see you again in two days time." Tabitha confirmed as she raised her hand to wave goodbye to her guide.

"Yes you shall. Be well," she answered back. With that, the figure in black made her exit, disappearing within the same cloud of black smoke and weak sparks that she arrived in.

2
The Story of Three

The figure in black arrived back in her own realm. She was in a room that was devoid of any detail or color—unless you would consider skull-white a color—and the room had no door or furnishings of any kind, save for a lone chair in the corner, and one window; a window she stared out of while deep in thought about something. In fact, it was someone who had gotten the wheels in her head spinning, spinning much too fast for her liking. For some reason, her recent visit with Tabitha Wilkinson had affected her deeply. So many questions the little girl had for her, and so unprepared was she to receive them. But she had begun to wonder what her story actually was. How did she come to be in this state? Who or what exactly killed her, if something or someone had killed her at all? Or perhaps she choked to death on a random food item in some random restaurant in some random town. She could have even drowned in the ocean while the sea life looked on, not lifting a finger or fin to help. Or maybe she had committed that one unspeakable act, the act of removing oneself from the life of the living, the act of suicide.

As she stared out into the billowing gray tufts of what resembled clouds that slowly passed in the area above her that could only be sky, she thought and thought to herself but nothing manifested. This affected her more than she anticipated. Perhaps a stroll would clear my mind, she thought, and she glided straight ahead, through the window and the wall that it was built into, and floated down to the ethereal plateau that resembled a ground. Many guides were leaving the premises in exactly the same fashion from windows next to, above and below hers and she observed every single one of them. She had known many of them for as long as she had been there, she did share the same dormitory after all, and ran into them from time to time, but this was the first time she had given any of them any thought.

When she landed, she paused for a moment, then turned and pondered her living quarters. It was great and tall, yet old fashioned in design. It was decrepit and it slanted from every side. It seemed as if it were going to collapse under the weight of whatever ghostly material that was used to build it—it strongly resembled rotting wood. Even trees come here when they die, she thought. This also caused other thoughts to come to her. She felt neither cold nor hot when in her quarters. When outside, she felt neither strong winds nor intense heat to compel her to hide from such conditions. Why then, did shelter exist in this realm at all?

She passed many of her peers on her afternoon stride. As she replied to the many *good afternoons* and *how are yous* that her contemporaries offered her as she strolled along, she could not help but stare and wonder—as she had never had before because she had no reason to—how they had all reached their ends.

One particular young looking male guide was pale in complexion, but other than this, had no visible signs of trauma. How had he died, she wondered? Maybe he perished peacefully in his sleep, a sickness perhaps?

Another, much older man, had a large gash in the side of his head, his face decorated with gobs of blood. Aside from this, he had a very cheerful expression, as he offered a smile as he passed her by. She gave a cordial nod. Surely he was murdered by meat cleaver, she had surmised.

The figure then studied a female guide who seemed to be in a hurry. The woman had her hair in a bun, displaying a rather large, red and blotchy bite wound on her neck. She remembered that she had once learned about the venom of snakes. The venom from a snake's bite did that one in, she thought very assuredly.

She then paused in her tracks once more, extremely startled by the fact that she was able to remember anything from her previous life at all. If she was able to remember arbitrary facts about snakes, let alone what a snake is in the first place, why then was she unable to remember something as monumental as the way she had died. The thoughts in her head were all too much to handle in an upright position and she felt the need to sit and ponder.

She approached a hill covered in decaying blades of what had once been grass, and scattered among the grass were gray stems and wilted petals of what used to be considered flowers, and upon this hill sat a long and decrepit piece of something that was once possibly called a log.

Upon the far end of this log sat three guides deep in conversation about something that she could not clearly hear. She had much rather had been alone, but the appeal of something to sit down on and think was too strong for her to ignore, so she sat on the far other end of the log and had chosen to ignore the guides instead. Upon sitting, she had noticed that she was facing a river of water. Did water come here when dead as well? She half thought. Then the other half of her thought remembered that she had not been as daft as to think such silly things as water dying. But she did not feel thirsty, nor did she feel the need for a nice, cool dip in a large body of water. Why then, was the reason for its existence here? As she watched, she began to see the bones of things that were most likely fish jumping in and out of the river. Interesting, she thought. Fish cannot walk so of course they would need water to swim in, and she was sure of how they came to be in this situation. People killed and ate fish; that much she was sure of. But more importantly, she still had no recollection of her own death.

She suddenly felt the familiar sensation of someone staring at her, and she turned her head to the left. The three guides had moved from their position at the far other end of the log and were now sat directly next to her, and after what seemed like an extremely awkward amount of time spent staring at one another, one of the guides finally spoke.

"Hello!" said the guide sat closest to the figure in black, enthusiastically. "And how are you today, my dear?"

"I'm quite well, thank you," she answered.

"Are you? You don't look well. You look quite the opposite," he said back bluntly.

"Who are you to judge what I am feeling?"

"I meant nothing by it, love. You just seem rather down and thought maybe there was something we could do about it. Cheer you up, perhaps."

"I don't need cheering up, thank you very much."

"Aww, love, we got off on the wrong foot. My apologies. Let's start over. Name's Nate, and these are my companions, Rowley and Jane."

Nate was tall and very lanky and sat with a great slump. His face was white, as was the usual complexion in these parts, and his hair was jet black and unruly. But his most distinguishing feature was the very large and very bloody hole in the middle of his forehead, and as the figure turned to face him, she could very clearly see Rowley and Jane through the large hole in Nate's head, and they very clearly saw her and waved. She waved back.

"Now, what seems to be the problem, love?" Nate asked. It seems he had taken a liking to calling her 'love.' She was not fond of that nickname, and the expression on her porcelain white face suggested her displeasure. She had much rather remained nameless than be called that, but she ignored it.

"Nothing," she answered, coldly.

"Come on now, maybe we can help. We're just trying to be friendly."

She thought for moment and then decided that they could probably provide her with some much-needed insight. And so she answered, "I cannot remember how I died, and it's bothering me quite a bit."

"What a shame. Absolutely shameful, that is," said Nate as he, Rowling, and Jane shook their heads in pity.

"Do you three remember your deaths?" she asked. Miss Wilkinson's inquisitiveness most definitely rubbed off on the figure in black.

"Why, I sure do, and so do they. Would you like to hear our stories? Maybe if you heard our stories, it could remind you of yours." The figure in black nodded.

"I'll go first," offered Nate.

"T'was tragic I tell ya. Right tragic and quite short. When I was alive I had a brother whom I loved and he loved me and he was quite young, eight or nine, I could never remember. And when I was alive, I had an affinity for guns. I had twelve of them. Of that

I could always remember. And then one day I checked for them and I had eleven of them. And when I searched my house for the missing one, I found my brother in the kitchen with the very loaded missing gun. And when I called out his name it startled him and he turned around and he blasted a hole clear through my head as big as a lime," Nate said as he pointed at the sizeable and bleeding wound in his head.

"And before I knew it, I was here in this lovely place, with this lovely lot, and here I am, sharing this story with you."

"Oh my, that is rather tragic," said the figure in black. The story gave her the sensation of sadness, and she would have cried if she could, but no tears formed in her eyes. Being dead eliminated the need to cry, she thought.

She then looked to Rowley, a bald figure with a bit of heft, but not so much as to be considered entirely fat. He also had a distinguishing feature, as every guide seemed to have: there was a small river of blood flowing from his mouth into his black robes, and he spat little specks of blood as he spoke.

"My story is also somewhat of a tragic one," he started.

"When I was alive I also had a brother and I also had a sister, and of course that would lead you to the belief that we also had a mother, and you would be correct to believe so. And I believed my mother to love me, and as such, I loved her deeply. And my mother, so religious was she that she always carried with her a book of her beliefs and a crucifix round her neck, and it pained her so that I was not as pious as she. Now, my siblings were quite younger than I, and she did not want me to influence them in a direction away from her beliefs. And with each passing year her enthusiasm for her religion became stronger and stronger, and with it her disdain for my reluctance to adhere to its rules. And with each passing year, she grew into a woman that was no longer the woman I knew and loved, but I still loved her with all of my heart."

"And so one day I come round for supper, and she served me mash, mash being my most favorite dish, and of course she knew this. She poured a heaping helping of beef gravy over the top of it, just how I liked it. Little did I know, the gravy was to mask the taste of the shards of glass she had mixed into my mash, ground not so finely as to resemble sand, but not left so large that I would notice, and definitely large enough to cut flesh. And as I looked at my mother I tried to ask why she had done this, but the blood that poured from my throat had impaired my ability to speak, and so I died face down in a bowl of my most favorite dish, made by my most favorite person that I believe had loved me."

The familiar feeling of sadness the story before his had brought to her had compounded, and if she hadn't known better, she could have sworn that an actual tear had fallen from her eye socket. But one did not.

"I'm sorry," was the only response she was able to give. She was much too choked up to say anything else.

She then looked at the figure sat to the left of Rowley.

"I'm sorry to say, but my story is no less tragic," said a high and incredibly scratchy voice, a voice that sounded like rusty nails on an old chalkboard; a voice that came from Jane. Jane sat slightly hunched over, her bloodshot eyes oddly wide in her face. Her hair was displayed as a long and dark brown braid wrapped around her thin and pasty neck like a large and hairy python snake.

"When I was alive I had a sister and we loved each other so," she spoke. "To say we were the best of friends would be a very true and accurate declaration. And when I was alive I had the same long hair as you see here, and I was the envy of many a female in my village because of it. And one day my sister became betrothed to a very handsome and strong young man, and on that day she became a woman consumed with jealousy, a trait she did not possess before this day, and it made her cold to me."

"And then one day her betrothed had admired my hair so and he complimented my braid and did so on many an occasion after. This did not please my sister, as you can imagine. And then one day, a vile and very untrue rumor was spread throughout the village by someone unknown that her betrothed had another, and that the other was no other than I. And my sister, being so blinded by love and jealousy, believed it without good evidence and began to hate me because of it. And then one night a shadow had crept quietly into my bedroom whilst I slept and very quietly crawled onto my bed where I lay asleep, and when I opened my eyes to see whom or what had crawled into my bed, I looked into the eyes of the woman whom I had loved very much and I believed loved me, and she slowly strangled me to death with my very own hair, conveniently wrapped in a braid."

By this time, the figure in black would have very much liked to shed a tear, and the thought of not being able to saddened her even more. She thought to dunk her head in the nearby river and fill her skull with water so that at least something resembling tears could trickle out of her sockets. She did not do this.

"Thank you for sharing your stories with me. They've touched me in a way I did not expect," said the figure in black.

"Is your memory properly jogged then?" asked Nate. She thought for a moment before sorrowfully shaking her head. With hands stroking their chins the three guides then each began to ponder ways she could have died. Rowley took a long look at the figure in black and snapped his fingers.

"That crack on your forehead most definitely has something to do with it," said Rowley. Nate and Jane nodded in agreement.

"Maybe you were bludgeoned to death with a baseball bat," he continued.

"No, that's definitely a cricket bat mark. Yep, a cricket bat done that," said Nate.

"Perhaps it was a hammer," squeaked Jane. "How positively idiotic. No hammer could have done that. Absolutely a cricket bat injury," reiterated Nate.

"Maybe someone threw a brick at her. The mark is rather red."

"I think that to be blood, Rowley. Besides, bricks used to come in all sorts of colors. Cricket bat I say," said Nate, adamantly.

Whether a red brick, a baseball bat or a cricket bat, none of this bickering had brought up any memories of how she had died.

"Thank you, but none of this is helping," said the figure in black as she stood to leave.

"It seems that you're unsatisfied with our speculations," said Nate.

"There is one individual who may be able to help," spoke Rowley.

"And who might that be?" asked the figure in black, and the three guides all pointed to a rather tall and rather black structure off in the distance.

"It is common knowledge that Death himself resides there," said Jane. "He would surely know your story."

"He would surely know indeed," added Rowley.

"You should visit him. I've heard no one visits. I would suspect he would appreciate the company," said Nate, rather unsurely.

"And why does no one visit him?" asked the figure. Nate shrugged.

"Who knows? No reason to, I suppose. I haven't had one. Have you two?" He posed the question to Rowley and Jane, and they shook their heads in unison.

"Then that is what I'll do," said the figure draped in black. "I shall pay him a visit. You have my gratitude, Nate, Rowley and Jane."

Before she left, Nate kindly asked, "And you, you've not told us your name, love. What is it?"

And the figure in black stood for a moment and briefly considered taking on the nickname Nate had bestowed upon her. Love. But, as she thought about the notion it made her shiver, and not in a pleasant way.

And so, she turned her head and simply answered, "I have no such thing," and with that, she made her way toward the structure in black in the distance, and the three guides returned to their conversation.

3
Death Himself

The figure in black arrived to the structure of a similar color, which sat on top of a small hill. It was a rather tall and thin structure. It was quite imposing and had no doors that could be spoken of. She was intimidated by it for sure, and hesitated for a moment before pushing her way through the black wall that stood before her.

Once inside, she was greeted by walls the color of pure tar on either side of her and matching flooring beneath her robes, and a great, long hall in front of her. At the end of this great hall was of course, the back of the structure; and built into the back of this structure was a lone window that was almost as thin and tall as the structure itself. It let in the eeriest grayish-white light from outside that shone against the back of a very tall figure sitting at a relatively normal sized desk, casting a very long shadow the length of the hall. Whoever it was seemed to be deep into what seemed like paperwork on the desk, but the figure at the desk soon noticed the figure in black and called out to her.

"Who goes there?" he asked in a low and booming voice, a voice that reverberated throughout the hall.

Before she could answer his inquiry, he said, "I jest. I know who goes there. Please, come forward," and the figure in black complied with his request.

The closer she got to him, the larger and larger he appeared, like a rapidly growing black tree that grew instantaneously before her. Soon, she was engulfed in the whole of his shadow, and because of the moderate amount of backlight, she was barely able to see the imposing figure that sat before her. But what she could see was a great figure that did indeed resemble a tree, a terrible old and frightening one draped in black, much more black than she wore; much more black than her tiny body would be capable of wearing. And near the top of this figure was a hooded white face: a face that resembled an aged and decaying and very wrinkled squash that had been left in a cupboard somewhere for much too long. But this squash had two black sockets where eyes should be and a mouth, a mouth that once again began to speak.

"Welcome. You have surprised me," said the talking squash. "I do not get visitors all too often. I wonder, what brings you here, my dear?" The name 'my dear' was much more preferable to 'love' she thought.

She wasn't quite sure how to address him, so she started, "Yes. Well, Death, sir…" but before she could continue, the large and imposing figure stood up, making himself even more large and more imposing, and leaned toward her so that he was face to face with her. She could feel fear rising in her body, but also knew that being afraid was of no use. Nothing could be worse than death, and she was already in that state, so why would she be fearful? But the figure that stood before her was so horrifying that he was able to instill fright in her in spite of this fact.

"My dear, that is not my name," said the large white and wrinkly face, in an unusually calm voice. "Death is what we, as guides, ease the living into, but I am not death itself, and I find the name to be quite offensive. It makes it sound as if I am the cause of death and I am most certainly not."

"My… my apolo…"

"…Nor am I called the Grim Reaper," he continued, cutting her off. "The name itself is, well, rather grim. Nor do I reap anything, especially, so that name as well is all around rather inaccurate if nothing else," he finished.

She waited for him to say more words, but he did not, and so she said, "I am sorry. It was not my intention to offend you."

"It is all right my dear. You did not know, but now you do, and I would prefer it if you never address me as such again. You may, however, continue to call me sir. Now, what brings you to me today?" he asked as he slowly returned to his seat.

"Well, sir," she began as she felt what seemed like a lump forming in her throat. "I have some… questions." The larger figure in black nodded, and the smaller figure took that as a sign to continue.

"I… I'm not quite sure of how I died, of how I came to be in this position or of what my name is or was and I have felt uneasy because of it." The imposing figure laughed and it echoed throughout the chamber.

"When the freshly dead come to us, we give them a speech regarding the details and rules of the occupation and send them on their way, nothing more and nothing less. And since they are dead they do not question a thing: nothing else matters. They know they died and now they are here. They accept it. But every so often I get someone like you, ones who cannot remember. The curious. But, I know your story, and it is quite special. I have come across many more special than yours, mind you, but that does not make yours any less interesting."

Extremely tall file cabinets surrounded him. They were quite taller than he, made of an off white material that may have been petrified wood or the finest marble, or even pumice perhaps, but was most likely bone. He outstretched his impossibly long arm that resembled a withered tree branch covered in tattered cloth, to the top most drawer on his right, opened it and brought down a file that bore resemblance to a tuft of smoke, placed it on the table and pushed it toward her.

As he interlocked his boney and withered fingers and rested his chin on top of this ghostly weave, he said, "This is your case. You may have a look if you wish."

She started to reach for it, but before she had the chance to lay a finger on it he spoke again.

"Within this file are the details of your death and your name. That would answer two of the three questions you had for me. The answer to your third is 'tragedy'." The small figure in black looked at him with confusion, and he took notice as he explained further.

"Tragedy brings you to us my dear," said he. "If one dies in a most horrible and tragic way, they are to join us as a guide to help us ferry those with the fortune of a more generous death to another existence."

"And why is tragedy the key, sir?" asked the small figure in black, as she fought through another lump.

"Tragic death is almost always immediate, and one that suffers from an instant death does not usually have the luxury of consultation with a guide, as you very well know." She nodded. "But they most certainly do have a caretaker, and that caretaker is I. But I cannot do this task alone. So, I thought it beneficial to employ you as helpers."

"So, I died tragically, sir?"

"That would be the implication, yes."

She grew quiet for a very long time before speaking anything else, and then she finally said, very boldly, "And how did you die sir, if I may ask?"

"You may ask, but I will not clearly answer," said the large and imposing figure in black. "The details of my death are either several hundred years old or several millennia old. It took place in either the 15th century or the 7th century. It might've taken place in a time before centuries were counted, but would you know the difference?"

She shook her tiny head. He continued.

"If I am entirely truthful, and I always am, I have forgotten some of the events that led to my demise, but I do remember most of them, and I cherish them and they are uniquely mine, and therefore would very much like to keep them very private. Is this answer satisfactory?"

She nodded.

"But I will share with you another tragedy that happened to me. Would you like to hear this story?" he asked, and she nodded once more.

His mouth started to move and words flowed from his wrinkled lips in the form of a poem, or at least that's how she started to hear it. But what she suddenly felt was not the sensation of listening, but the sensation of being; she felt as if she were a participant of his story; a story that went like this:

Once upon a lifetime, of whose I will not say, but it may very well be my own,
I did a fair bit of ferrying and I did it all alone.
And one day, I came across a farmer, very old yet still very able,

As he worked with a scythe in his hands on a field of crops of some unknown staple.

And he saw me and welcomed me with open arms and he asked, 'Is it my time?'

And I answered truthfully, as I always do, 'Yes, I am afraid it is. You are well past your prime.'

And ready was he, but before he perished wanted to have one last conversation,

So he asked me to listen, and listen I did, without hesitation.

And he told me of his family, the members of which had passed well before him and whom he loved a lot,

And he told me of all his dreams and all his nightmares, and which of which came true and which did not.

He told me his beliefs and some were silly and some weren't quite,

But a silly one was one of a dragon he had seen that he thought was an exquisite sight.

We had spoken for hours and with no one around to grieve,

He exclaimed to me that he was now quite ready to leave.

And as he lay down he confessed to me of his dying wish, to die with his trusty scythe at his side,

And he folded his arms with a final breath and he closed his eyes and died.

And as per the farmer's last wish, I picked up his tool,

But before I could lay it down beside him another came and screamed at the sight of me, he screamed like a fool.

And so, with tool in hand, I made a hasty retreat,

And now I am forever known as the terrifying skeleton in a hood with a scythe, and with that, my story is complete.

Her senses returned to her, and she was once again simply standing within the shadow of a large and dark figure in a large and dark room, and she said, "That was a lovely story, but if you'll forgive me for saying, sir, I fail to recognize the tragedy in that."

"Well, you see my dear, before this no one had seen me except those who were to die. And I sympathized with this farmer, and because of it I lingered for far too long. And because I lingered I was seen very briefly by someone who was very much alive, and the story of my incorrect visage spread throughout the years. And now I appear in literature and in songs and in people's visions and in people's nightmares as something to be feared, as something dreadful and horrendous, and I like to think of myself as anything but. I know I may not look it, but I am kind and I am loving. I was so in my former life and am so now. It was from that day forward that I began to employ the souls of those that died tragically, for I could no longer ferry myself for the fear of being accidentally seen again."

"I now see the tragedy in that, sir. I see it very plainly," she said so truthfully. She looked to his left and noticed a long stick with a long and curved blade attached to it leaning against the windowsill that reminded her of the bones of a bird that might have possibly lived at one time or another.

"And is that a souvenir?" she asked of it.

"That is indeed," he said as he turned and looked at the scythe that once belonged to an old farmer—that was now his—with deep sorrow. "A reminder of that day."

"And this sir, may I finally have a look at it?" And she moved for the smoky file on his desk, but he grabbed it and put it back in its place in the cabinet most likely made of bone.

"I'm sorry. My story seemed to have taken up all of your time. The other answers will have to wait for another occasion. I believe you are due to collect a Miss Wilkinson."

The small figure in black lifted her head as if she smelled something rotten in the air, or as if she had heard a strange voice in her ear, then turned her attention once again to the dark figure incorrectly identified as Death and said, "You are most correct sir. I shall make my leave now. I thank you for your time."

"You are most welcome my dear. And I thank you for your visit. You may come again," he answered back. "I hope you find your story."

She nodded her head and suddenly disappeared in a flurry of sparks and a cloud of dense black smoke as the figure at the desk returned to his work.

4
A Story of Her Own

One gloomy morning, the figure in black appeared once again in the small yet spacious bedroom of one, Miss Tabitha Wilkinson. Sunlight forced its way through the stubbornly thick clouds and shone through the window illuminating everything that she wasn't able to see on her previous visit. The walls of the room were a faint shade of pink and covered with the amateurish, yet quite adept, drawings of a child, and on the left side of the window sat a great big white wardrobe dresser that looked older than the room it now sat in. On the left side of the room sat a set of beds: one that was properly made that looked as if it hadn't been touched for quite some time, and the other had a small hump in the middle of it surrounded by machines that beeped and hissed. Protruding from the small hump in the bed was a bald and frail head, a head the figure recognized as the one belonging to Miss Wilkinson.

She cleared her throat as she had done the time before, and quietly called out, "Miss Wilkinson, Tabitha Wilkinson."

The bald and sallow head slightly rose, and as her sunken eyes had met with the familiar black sockets of the figure in black, she pepped up as much as one in her condition could.

"Guide, you're...you're back," said Miss Wilkinson in a weak and tiny voice as she coughed and wheezed and coughed some more. "Has it been two days already?"

"I believe it has been, at least here it has. There is no concept of time where I am from," said the figure in black.

"Then..." Tabitha coughed again. "...Then how do you know when it's time to come?" she asked innocently.

"We just know," answered the figure in black, very vaguely. "Have you been well?"

Tabitha sat up in her bed, and as she did so the expression on her face looked as if she were being stabbed in the back by many sharp knives. Several wires connected to the several machines were stuck to her arms and face in every which way. It looked, the figure in black thought, extremely uncomfortable.

"I've been trying to be, I really have been. But I've been unsuccessful," she said. "The doctors said that I've gotten much worse unexpectedly. But I expected it of course." A combination of a laugh and a cough left her mouth. "My mum and dad say that if I don't get better by today, I'll have to go to back to the hospital. But since you're here now, I guess I won't be."

"I hope you've made the proper good byes," said the guide. "Are you ready?"

"Is this it? You just come and we just leave?" asked Tabitha, genuinely surprised at this revelation. More coughs followed.

"Yes. This is the general procedure."

"Oh guide, I would very much like to have one last conversation. Besides, you owe me a story," and Tabitha patted the spot next to her on the bed with her weak and skinny hand, and the figure in black looked at Miss Wilkinson's bedroom door with apprehension before slowly taking a seat at her side.

"And did you find out your name and why you are a guide and how you died?" asked Tabitha, visibly weak yet visibly excited to hear the answers. But the figure in black could not help but disappoint her.

"I did not find out what I was called and I did not find out the cause of my death, but I did find out why I am what I am,"

"And why is that?"

"I died tragically, and those who die tragically are duty-bound to perform this task," said the figure.

"Tragedy," Tabitha whispered as she wheezed and coughed and wheezed some more. "Well, I did a bit of research on your kind since the last time you were here, guide,"

"Oh, did you now?" the figure in black asked with genuine interest.

"Yes I did," Tabitha said as she successfully fought back a cough. "And do you know what you are known as here?" asked Tabitha and the figure shook her head no.

"You are known as a 'Psychopomp.' And since you do not yet know your name, I wanted to give you one. And my question to you is which do you prefer? Psycho or Pomp?" said Tabitha, and she sweetly laughed, then not quite so sweetly wheezed. A curl formed in the guide's mouth; a curl that resembled a smile.

"That was my attempt at humor. I'm sorry if it wasn't amusing."

"It was, Miss Wilkinson. And for the record, I prefer neither."

"Then we'll have to think up another for you."—A cough and a wheeze—"If you'll excuse me, I think I want to lie down again," said Tabitha as she coughed a little cough and made her way beneath her blankets once more.

"And did you have anything else you wanted to talk about, Miss Wilkinson?" the figure in black cautiously asked, anxious to get a move on.

"Yes. Do you mind if I tell you a story?"

The figure again looked at the bedroom door, then back to Miss Wilkinson then back to the door once more. She didn't want to risk being seen by anyone, especially anyone alive, but she also did not want to refuse what could have been a last request, and so she answered, quite simply, "Yes" and Tabitha continued with her story.

"I've never told anyone this. Not even my parents." She paused before she spoke again. "I once had a sister you know," said Tabitha.

"Oh?"

"Yes, I had a twin sister and loved her so. We were inseparable. We did everything together. We played together, we ate together, we studied together, and we read together. We did it all but bathe together because that's just weird,"—A laugh and a cough—"And she was ever so much smarter than I, and much more artistic. While I played with silly dolls, she would draw pictures, hundreds of lovely pictures. She was always with colored markers or pencils in hand."

The coughs and wheezes were becoming more violent and more frequent and now sounded faintly of chainsaws and dying cats. But she continued on.

"And then one day, while watching television we saw a show about festivals from around the world from places like America and Brazil and China. And in some of these places all of these fabulous men and women were dancing and wearing the most vibrant and colorful costumes and decorated masks. My sister was drawn to the masks in particular. And then one day our mum and dad surprised us with random presents: more dolls for me, of course, and a new paint set for her. And for canvases for her to paint on, they bought her dozens…" —a strong cough followed by a very painful sounding wheeze— "…dozens of, of plain white masks. And she painted on these masks and tried her best to copy what she had seen on television."

Her breathing had become much more labored and it seemed that every single word that she spoke caused her much pain. The figure in black suddenly had a strange urge to comfort the small, frail girl that lied before her, but she did not know how to accomplish this, and so she only said, "No need to continue." But Tabitha put up a hand to signal that she could and that she would.

"One day, my sister sat right on that windowsill thinking of what to draw on her next mask while I twirled in place trying to make myself dizzy for no other reason than I am a stupid girl. She then placed the mask on her face and asked me what I thought she should paint. So I stopped twirling to answer her, but I was much too dizzy and could not stand straight and I toppled right into my sister who was sitting at the windowsill with the window wide open, and I accidentally pushed her out of it, and that was the last time I saw my sister alive," said Tabitha.

She then grabbed the guide's hand and in an instant, memories suddenly and rapidly filled the figure's head: memories of markers and pencils, and of masks and paint; memories of pillow fights and tickle fights and nice warm baths; memories of books with words and drawings, and of plates with cakes; memories of laughs and tears and of hugs and kisses; memories of a mum and a dad and most vividly, of a sister; a sister that she loved with all of her heart; then lastly, a memory of falling, a memory of hitting pavement, and then nothing. Her hand then wandered to the mysterious crack in her forehead, no longer mysterious of course, and as she touched it the tears that she once wished she had were now suddenly overflowing uncontrollably from her black eye sockets as she realized the truth: she was the very sister Miss Tabitha Wilkinson spoke of.

"My poor parents believed it to be an accident, but I could not tell them the truth. I just couldn't. I believed they would have hated me for it," said Tabitha. Her coughs and wheezes were now mixed with sobs and tears.

"You know, now that I see you in a much better light guide, you look very familiar. In fact, your face resembles…" Tabitha trailed off, and then she said, "Please guide, please look in that wardrobe," and the guide wiped her face and complied.

She stood up and opened the wardrobe doors, and as she did she was greeted with rows and rows of colorful masks lining the backsides of the wardrobe doors: some blue, some red, some with drawings of cats and birds, others with drawings of stars and moons, all with strings dangling from them, all filled to their edges with color. The guide's face was flooded with tears once more as the vivid memories of painting the masks flooded her mind.

"Lovely aren't they? Your face reminds of them. What an odd coincidence," said Tabitha, and the guide nodded.

Tabitha, now barely able to talk, managed a few more words.

"Guide…" —her breath was all but gone— "…Guide, do you think my sister forgives me?" she asked hopefully with the most strength she had left. The guide turned and approached Tabitha, and stroked her bald little head and said, "She most certainly does," and Tabitha managed to smile for a final time.

"Guide, please lay with me. I feel cold," and the guide once again did as she was told.

"Guide?"

"Yes Tabitha?" she said, as she lied next to her. She could feel Tabitha's small body becoming colder with every passing second.

"My sister's name was Agatha. So I think I'll give that name to you. Do you like it?" And a final memory had entered the figure's mind. The memory of her real name that began and ended with the letter A: Agatha.

"Yes I do, very much indeed," answered the guide, now identified as Agatha.

With her last dying breath, Tabitha mustered one last question. "Will I ever see you again, guide?"

The guide knowing the answer but not wanting to say said nothing, and simply wrapped her arms around her sister and snuggled in closer embracing her for a final time. With that, Tabitha and Agatha Wilkinson both closed their eyes and said nothing more.

And the guide was happy that she now finally had, tragic as it might be, a story of her very own.

THE END

About the Author:

K. N. Parker is a simple man in his thirties, and was born and raised in Los Angeles, California. He is currently working on a full-length novel and two more short stories. He shares heritages with two countries: America and Japan, and he spends his time between the two whenever possible. When in his late teens he thought it proper to teach himself Japanese, and so he did, and now can communicate with you in two ways, if applicable. When not writing or creating trouble in various coffee shops throughout the world, he enjoys graphic design, television, and film.

Connect with Me Online:

E-Mail: kiyoshiparker@gmail.com

My Blog: http://kiyoshiparker.blogspot.com/

Twitter: http://twitter.com/KiyoshiParker

Facebook: http://www.facebook.com/deathexists

Facebook Author Page: https://www.facebook.com/authorKNParker

CPSIA information can be obtained
at www.ICGtesting.com
Printed in the USA
LVOW04s1609130616

492390LV00050B/1992/P